THE CIRCLE OF DEATH INCIDENT

TERRANCE DICKS

THE CIRCLE OF DEATH INCIDENT

Piccadilly Press • London

Terrance Dicks lives in North London. He has written many books
for Piccadilly Press including the CHANGING UNIVERSE series
and the SECOND SIGHT series.

Cover design by Judith Robertson

PROLOGUE

It was surprisingly easy to break into the Holy Place.

He came by night, long after all the gaping fools of tourists had gone home. Despite the enormous importance of his sacred mission, his transport was humble enough. He rode the battered old black bicycle he'd been using for years. In any event, it was all he could afford – the way of the prophet is hard in an uncaring, modern world. The ancient machine had been carefully oiled, so that its usual creaks and groans were silenced.

In his long, flapping, white robes, hood pulled down over his face, he glided silently through the night like some giant white moth.

There were no lights on the bicycle and the headlights of approaching cars were easy enough to see. There weren't too many at this hour, and whenever a car came near he stopped cycling and got off the road, waiting in the shadows until the car had passed by.

At last he reached the fence that ran round the perimeter of the sacred site – the blasphemous modern fence that barred the true believers from the Holy Place. It was an ordinary wire-netting affair, the sort of thing you might find in a garden centre, not much higher than a reasonably tall man.

He rode along the edge of the fence until the looming shape of the outer Heel Stone gave him his bearing. Dismounting, he unstrapped the saddlebag from the bike and threw it over the fence. After that it was a simple matter to lean his bicycle against the fence, climb up on to the saddle and tumble over to the other side.

He looked around carefully, alert for any sign of the site security men. He knew that the stones were guarded day and night, but there was no sign of anyone now. He'd been too clever for them.

He stood by the jagged Heel Stone for a moment, looking reverently at the dark shapes of the great stone circle, outlined against the night sky. Wind sighed eerily across the open plain.

Picking up his saddlebag, he set off for the Altar Stone in the centre of the ring. But, before he even reached the sacred circle, he stopped in sudden alarm. A figure was moving some way away in the darkness, over by one of the Station Stones that stand outside the main ring. He stood still, watching. Was it a guard? Surely not. There was a stealth about the other's movements that matched his own. This was another unauthorised invader.

He saw the figure crouch down. The dark shape was digging!

Forgetting that he was an illegal intruder himself, the tall old man in the druid's robes strode forward. His respect for the sacred place was passionately sincere. This was blasphemy!

He ran towards the figure. 'Stop!' he boomed. 'Stop that at once! How dare you profane the sacred stones!'

The shape beside the Station Stone arose. It was tall and incredibly thin, with glowing green eyes, and even at this distance the old man could see that it wasn't human.

The old man stood frozen in horror for a

moment. The tall shape stretched out a long, slender arm in a curious pointing gesture.

A thin beam of light shot out, and the old man found himself in the agonising grip of some incredible force. He gave a single scream of terror, then the energy beam slammed him backwards on to a fallen stone close by, cracking his skull against the half-buried stone.

The tall shape turned to resume its work, but the old man's dying scream had been heard. Uniformed figures pounded towards him, there were shouts and the beams of torches cutting through the night. The figure vanished into the darkness.

When the security guards arrived, all they found was the dead body of the old druid, sprawled out on the ground. Blood from his shattered skull trickled across the surface of the Slaughter Stone.

Chapter One

THE SACRED STONES

'Stonehenge?'

Professor James Stirling, head of the Scientific Research Institute's Department of Paranormal Studies, gave me one of his well-known withering glares. It was a look which had been known to reduce nervous research students to quivering jellies. However, since the grumpy old devil also happens to be my father – I'm Matt Stirling – I'd been glared at so often that I was just about wither-proof.

Dad runs the Department of Paranormal Studies pretty well single-handed, and I'm his unofficial assistant. Professionally and personally, it's a relationship that has its problems.

Mum and Dad split up when I was still a baby, and Dad went to work in America. After Mum died I was brought up by relatives. When they retired and went to live abroad, Dad was landed with a son he hardly knew, and I had a totally unknown father on my hands.

At about the same time, Dad's research funds dried up – he's a top space research scientist – and he was more or less shanghaied into the Paranormal Studies post. Deciding to make the best of things, he took me out of school and made me his assistant. He told the authorities that he was educating me himself and, since he's got degrees in almost everything, no one dared argue.

Since then, my life has become a lot more interesting – and downright terrifying at times. Working with Dad isn't always easy. He's arrogant, bad-tempered and obstinate – and that's on his good days.

According to him, I'm stubborn, opinionated and lack respect for my elders and betters – meaning him.

From time to time there's a certain amount of friction – not to mention the occasional blazing row. All in all though, we don't get along too badly. In fact, we're really quite fond of each other, though neither of us would ever admit it.

Dad is pretty much a sceptic about the

paranormal, which isn't a bad attitude for an investigator. I like to think I'm more open-minded. We've already investigated two incidents involving aliens and UFOs, one in Australia, the other in the Bermuda Triangle, off the coast of Florida. Since then Dad has become rather less sceptical, and I am even more open-minded than before.

Things had been quiet since our return from America and I'd got pretty fed up with sitting around in our top-floor Hampstead flat doing a strict course of lessons devised and marked by Dad. I'd have been better off at school. At least there'd have been company, and the odd games period to break the monotony.

In my spare time, I'd been looking around for some project to justify our existence – or rather, the existence of the Department of Paranormal Studies.

The choice had been surprisingly easy. I did some research, which made me more interested than ever. A few days later, I went and tackled Dad in his study.

He was writing an article for *New Scientist*, arguing that civilisation as we know it was doomed unless the space programme was re-instated at once, preferably with unlimited funds and him in charge.

He resented being interrupted, and he wasn't very impressed by my suggestion for a new project.

'What on earth is there to investigate about Stonehenge? It's been sitting there on Salisbury Plain for a thousand years.'

'Five thousand years, actually,' I said. 'Archae-ologists reckon construction started at about three thousand BC. That was just the circular ditch and the bank. The first stones arrived in around two thousand-six-hundred BC – bluestones from Preseli Mountain in Wales. Two or three hundred years later they brought the sarsen-stones from Marlborough Downs, about thirty kilometres away . . .'

'All right, all right, five thousand years,' said Dad irritably. He hates it when I know more about something than he does. 'What's all this got to do with us? We're supposed to investigate the para-normal, remember? We're not archaeologists.'

Before I could answer he was off again. 'And don't you dare give me any of that nonsense about the ancient druids and their mystic powers, either.'

'Oh?' I asked innocently. 'Why not? What have you got against druids? You'd probably have been one yourself in the old days.'

I could just see him prancing about in white robes at the midsummer festival.

'Stonehenge has got nothing to do with druids,' snarled Dad. 'It's a popular misconception. The druids were a Celtic priesthood around the time of the Roman conquest. And you said yourself, Stonehenge was built thousands of years before that.'

I knew from my own research that he was almost certainly right. Just to wind him up, I said innocently, 'Lots of people still believe that Stonehenge was originally a druid temple.'

'The druids didn't *have* temples,' snapped Dad. 'They held all their ceremonies in clearings in the forest. All that Stonehenge as a druid temple nonsense was dreamed up by some eighteenth-century archaeologist.'

'Quite right,' I said. 'The Ancient Order of Druids was actually founded in 1781.'

'There you are,' said Dad triumphantly. 'Why

drag in the druids, then?'

'I wasn't going to,' I said cheerfully. 'You brought them up yourself, remember?'

Dad drew a deep breath. 'In that case . . .'

'Druids apart, Stonehenge has always been associated with the paranormal. Take ley lines, for instance.'

Dad snorted. 'You take them! Mysterious lines of force criss-crossing the country . . .'

'Two of the most important ley lines intersect at Stonehenge,' I said. 'There's a report about a researcher who pointed a special aerial at Stonehenge from hundreds of metres away – and got blasted off his feet by a mysterious energy surge. His arm didn't recover for six months.'

Dad didn't look convinced.

'Then there are all the UFO sightings,' I went on.

Dad groaned. 'Well, I prefer UFOs to druids. Been landing at Stonehenge, have they?'

'There have been several recorded sightings through the years. In 1968, an observer saw what he called a "ring of fire" taking off from the actual stones. In 1977, a whole formation of glowing lights was seen hovering over the stone circle. In

14

fact, UFOs have been seen all over the area. Have you heard about Warminster?'

'What about it?'

'Little town in Wiltshire. It's been called the UFO capital of England. More recorded sightings than almost anywhere else.'

'What's that got to do with Stonehenge?'

'Warminster is halfway between Stonehenge and Glastonbury – which is just about the most sacred ancient site in Britain. The UFOs seem to follow a flight corridor between Glastonbury and Stonehenge, which brings them directly over Warminster.'

'Why?' demanded Dad. 'Why should UFOs spend their time buzzing up and down between Glastonbury and Stonehenge?'

'Stonehenge is surrounded by all kinds of restricted areas,' I said. 'Secret installations run by the Army and the Air Force. Maybe they're just keeping an eye on us. Taking care we don't develop too many nasty weapons.'

Dad sighed. 'Is that it?'

'I'm just getting started,' I said. 'I haven't even mentioned the astronomical side. A professor at Harvard used an IBM computer to prove that

Stonehenge has a pattern of lunar and solar alignments. He reckoned it's a kind of Neolithic computer that could be used to predict eclipses of the moon. Maybe it was used for other astronomical calculations as well.'

'Maybe so,' said Dad. 'I know a bit about the astronomical side, and some of the work that's been done is very interesting. But most of the paranormal stuff is speculation, hearsay and rumour – with a strong element of downright lunacy. If there was any hard, scientific evidence, I . . .'

'Oh come on, Dad,' I said impatiently. 'If it was all cut and dried there'd be nothing for us to investigate. All paranormal research is sifting through what you call hearsay and rumour – not to mention a certain amount of lunacy. And besides . . .'

'Besides what?'

'I know you hate to admit it, but we've had experiences of our own with aliens. Once in Australia, at Corroboree Rock, once in the Bermuda Triangle. Those experiences suggest that aliens have been visiting Earth for thousands of years, that we've only just started noticing them.'

'Go on,' said Dad seriously.

'Those other visits were associated with ancient sacred sites, places with a mysterious and supernatural reputation. Like Corroboree Rock out in Australia and the Bermuda Triangle itself. After all, there's nothing much older and more sacred than the sea. Now, if you were looking for a place that fitted that description right here in England . . .'

'You couldn't do much better than Stonehenge,' said Dad slowly. 'All right, Matthew, you've made your point. Let me have your research material and I'll take a look at it. If I'm convinced, we'll set up a project. Now, I really must finish this article.'

'Right. I'll get the material to you in a couple of days. Once you've read it we really ought to get moving.'

Dad was already turning back to his article. 'What's your hurry?' he grunted. 'Stonehenge has been standing there for five thousand years – it'll wait for a few more weeks!'

I hesitated in the doorway and Dad snapped, 'Well?'

'Look, I know this will sound crazy – especially to you. But I didn't exactly choose Stonehenge –

it's more as if it has chosen me. I've got a feeling that something is about to happen there – that we shouldn't waste any time.'

Dad snorted and I decided to quit while I was still ahead.

As I left the study, the phone rang. Irritably, Dad snatched it up. 'Professor Stirling! Who? What? *What*? Are you serious?'

The call didn't seem to be doing very much for his mood. I tiptoed out of the study.

I went into the kitchen, filled the kettle and switched it on. I could hear Dad's voice on the phone through the study door. His call was a fairly long one. As soon as he'd finished, the phone rang again and that call was followed by another.

This time Dad sounded calmer, and there was something in his tone that told me he was talking to someone important.

I was pouring boiling water on to my tea bag when Dad came into the room. He stood there for a moment, looking strangely at me.

'What is it?' I asked.

'You know, Matthew, I'm beginning to be convinced.'

'About Stonehenge?'

He shook his head. 'About the paranormal – and more specifically, about you! Have you shown any signs of prescience before?'

I stared at him. 'Signs of what?'

'Prescience. Precognition. Seeing the future!'

'Not as far as I know. Stop messing about, Dad. What's happened?'

'That call was from the Institute – the Ministry of Defence has requested our services. The second call was from the Ministry – someone called Alexander in Security.'

I strained my tea bag. 'Go on.'

'You know you had a feeling something was going to happen? Well, something has.'

'What?' I yelled. 'Are you going to tell me or not?'

'They've found a dead druid,' said Dad slowly. 'Skull shattered, body crushed by some unknown force.'

'At Stonehenge?'

He nodded. 'Lying on something they call the Slaughter Stone . . .'

Chapter Two

DEAD DRUID

Less than a hour later we were barrelling down the M3, heading for Stonehenge. One of the perks of Dad's job is the car of his choice, and for some reason he'd chosen a massive off-road vehicle called the Kamikaze Land Tourer. It is bright red, huge and high and extremely uncomfortable to ride in. No doubt the makers thought things like springs and suspension were cissy.

It would probably be invaluable on an expedition to the Gobi Desert, but in London it's pretty much of an embarrassment. On the other hand, since Dad drives as if nobody else has any right to be on the road at all, it's reassuring to be inside something that is built like a tank.

To go with the vehicle, Dad was wearing a huge safari jacket and a kind of bush hat. I think he thought he was Indiana Jones. Dad can be very childish sometimes.

I'd settled for jeans, hiking boots and a simple anorak.

'We're only going a few hours' drive from London, you know,' I said, when I saw his outfit. 'Why all the explorer's gear?'

'Stonehenge *is* in the open air, I believe,' said Dad acidly. 'No doubt we'll be spending a great deal of time poking around in damp grass and mud. It's late autumn, the sky is dark and there is rain in the air. I'm not all that fond of the great outdoors, but if I have to spend time in the open I like to be appropriately dressed.'

The vehicle and Dad's outfit attracted quite a few stares from passing drivers and the occasional rude comment.

'Don't worry, Dad,' I said. 'It's just jealousy. I expect they think you're David Attenborough setting off on another expedition to the uncharted jungles of Borneo or somewhere . . .'

It was quite a relief when we left the motorway and turned off on to the smaller roads leading to Stonehenge.

'Well, there it is,' I said at last.

There was the circle of stones, outlined against a dark and cloudy sky.

Stonehenge stands at the top of a small rise in the middle of Salisbury Plain. These days it's surrounded by a wire-netting fence. There's a carpark on the other side of the little road that runs alongside. The visitors' entrance is at the end of the carpark, and you reach the circle of stones by way of a tunnel under the road.

Dad swung our vehicle into the carpark entrance and a policeman stepped forward with upraised hand.

'Sorry, sir, Stonehenge is closed at the moment. There's been an accident. There's a very interesting Bronze Age monument at Woodhenge, not far away, and, of course, you're quite close to Salisbury.'

He rattled this off at a great rate as if he'd said it lots of times before.

When Dad didn't move the policeman said, 'Now come along, sir, you heard what I said. Stonehenge is closed.' He looked wearily up at Dad, obviously wondering if he was dealing with some exceptionally eccentric foreign traveller. 'You do speak English, mate?' he said sharply.

'I do indeed, mate,' said Dad, equally sharply. 'I'm waiting for the chance to do so.' He produced a pass and handed it down to the policeman. 'I am Professor Stirling from the Scientific Research Institute. I think you'll find I'm expected.'

The policeman studied the pass suspiciously and handed it back. 'One moment, sir.' He took a few steps away and spoke into a walkie-talkie. Then he came back to the car and said grudgingly, 'They do seem to be expecting you, sir. You can go through.'

Dad started the car and the policeman held up his hand again. 'I said *you* can go through, sir. Nothing was said about the boy.'

'The boy, officer, is my son, Matthew Stirling. He is also my assistant, and if he doesn't go in, I don't go in.'

The policeman hesitated and Dad snapped, 'Well? You can either let us go in or explain my immediate departure to your superiors.'

A tall, dark-haired man in a black trench-coat came hurrying up.

'Professor Stirling?'

'That is correct.'

'Chief Inspector Blane, Special Branch. Thank

you for coming down so quickly.'

'I shall be going back equally quickly unless you can persuade this officer to let me and my assistant in.'

Blane said, 'Let them both through, constable, I'll take responsibility.' The policeman nodded and stepped back.

Blane pointed. 'You can park over there, professor, by the entrance.'

Dad drove up close to the ticket-booth and parked. I saw two police cars and a police van, an ambulance and a couple of other vehicles, but, apart from that, the carpark was empty.

Blane came up as we got out of the car. 'If you'll come this way, sir?'

He led us towards a little group standing by the gate. 'Professor Stirling, ladies and gentlemen,' he said. 'This is his assistant, Matthew Stirling.'

One by one he introduced the rest of the group.

First, a stocky, grey-haired man in a fawn raincoat. 'Inspector Parker, from the local police.'

Next, a tall, white-haired man of distinction in an expensive overcoat. 'Doctor Saville, Police Surgeon.'

Then, a tough-looking, square-jawed character

in army uniform. 'Major Truscott, Military Intelligence.'

'Ah, Military Intelligence – oof!' said Dad.

The first bit was because he was about to trot out one of his favourite sayings – the one about 'Military Intelligence' being a contradiction in terms.

The 'oof' was because I'd jabbed him in the ribs with my elbow to shut him up.

Converting his 'oof' to a cough, Dad said, 'And this lady?' He nodded towards an intent-looking, bespectacled woman in a smart suit, who completed the small circle.

'Ah yes,' said Blane hurriedly. 'This is Ms Alexander from Security.'

'Yes, of course,' said Dad. 'We spoke on the telephone.'

'I'm afraid I'm the person responsible for dragging you down here, Professor Stirling,' said Ms Alexander apologetically. 'Mr Simmonds, my American colleague, gave me a full account of your valuable services in the Bermuda Triangle affair. And this must be your son Matthew!'

She beamed at me – unlike all the others, who'd ignored me – and we shook hands.

Simmonds had been the man in charge in Miami. He was high up in some mysterious intelligence outfit called the Agency.

I supposed that this meant that Ms Alexander was also a top spook. She didn't look very much like the spy type. More like a woman from a big solicitors, or city firm. But then, in the real world, being the sort of person who wouldn't stand out in a crowd could be quite a big advantage for a spy.

Dad looked around the little group. 'A formidable assembly,' he said. 'May I ask why one death is attracting quite so much high-powered attention?'

There was an awkward silence. It was broken by Chief Inspector Blane, who seemed to be the spokesman for all the others.

'Inspector Parker and Doctor Saville are here in the course of their normal duties . . .'

'Which they would very much like to be allowed to get on with,' said Doctor Saville.

Ignoring him, Dad said, 'And the rest of you? Our friends from – what is it you like to call yourselves? The Intelligence Community?'

'Anything   concerning   Stonehenge   is

potentially sensitive in intelligence terms,' said Blane. 'If only because of its position.'

'Firing ranges and tank training grounds all round,' said Major Truscott gruffly. 'Secret weapons establishments.'

'Not to mention such sensitive areas as Porton Down,' said Ms Alexander quietly. 'And certain other even more secret establishments that we don't like to talk about.'

Porton Down is Britain's centre for chemical and biological warfare. Anywhere more secret than that would be very secret indeed.

I wondered what other secrets were hidden in the area. I knew that the Ministry of Defence owned a surprising amount of the land around Stonehenge, and much of it was prohibited to the public. Even so, the explanations didn't seem quite satisfactory to me.

'But that's not all, is it?' I said.

Everybody stared at me as if surprised to discover that I could actually talk.

'I mean, it isn't enough,' I said. 'Not to justify a turn-out like this. There's something else. Something nobody wants to mention.'

'Matthew is referring to the question of

extraterrestrial involvement,' said Dad. 'That's why *we're* here, isn't it, ladies and gentlemen? Because of our experiences at Wollagong, and in the Bermuda Triangle.'

Chief Inspector Blane looked at Ms Alexander as if for permission to speak, and suddenly it was clear who was the real boss.

'You're quite right,' said Ms Alexander. 'There has been an increased amount of UFO activity recently, all focused on Stonehenge.'

'Have you any idea why?' asked Dad.

'None at all. As always, the motives of our alien visitors remain mysterious.' She paused. 'As I'm sure you know, the public's ideas of a kind of UFO cover-up conspiracy are both right and wrong. We don't have any crashed or shot-down UFOs, or any captured aliens, dead or alive. Nor do our American friends. What we do have is convincing evidence that alien spacecraft have been visiting Earth with increasing frequency since World War Two.' She looked hopefully at us both. 'If my suspicions are correct, we're in an area where you two have more experience than anyone here.'

'Strictly speaking, it's Matthew who has the experience,' said Dad, and everyone looked at me with renewed interest. 'Nevertheless, we will both help in any way we can.'

I looked hard at Major Truscott. 'You've really no idea why there's been all this alien activity? You've done nothing to provoke it? You haven't done anything recently, held any weapon tests that could be seen as some kind of attack?'

I was thinking about the Bermuda Triangle business, where the aliens had been understandably stirred up by people dropping atomic torpedoes on their undersea bases. If the Army had been testing some new secret weapon on passing UFOs, if they'd even made a serious effort to shoot one down . . .

Truscott shook his head. 'Nothing of the kind, I promise you.'

'I can confirm that,' said Ms Alexander. 'All we know is that something is going on here, but we don't know what, or why. We've almost been expecting an incident at Stonehenge.'

'Something like this?' I asked. 'A dead druid?'

'Not exactly,' said Ms Alexander wryly. 'But there are unusual features about this death; Doctor Saville will explain.'

'I should be happy to – given the opportunity,'

said Saville.

'Then let's get on with it,' said Dad.

We marched through the little tunnel and out on to the open viewing area beyond. There were the circles of stones, the outer circle, now largely ruined, enclosing the inner horseshoe.

Disappointingly small from a distance, Stonehenge grew more and more impressive as we drew closer.

On a half-buried stone, some way outside the circle, lay a crumpled white shape. Doctor Saville led us towards it, and we stood grouped around it in a semicircle.

Sprawled across the stone lay a scrawny, white-bearded, white-haired old man in a hooded white cloak. The body seemed shrunken, wizened somehow, and blood from the shattered skull was drying on to the rock.

'For some reason they call this the Slaughter Stone,' said Inspector Parker. 'They say it still runs red with the blood of the sacrificed victims whenever it rains.'

'It probably does if there are iron oxides in the stone,' said Dad. 'No doubt that's what gave rise to the ridiculous idea that it was a sacrificial altar.

It seems much more likely that it once stood upright like the others. More of this druid nonsense.'

'It looks as if *he* believed in it,' I said, looking down at the white-robed figure on the stone.

'Lots of people do,' said Inspector Parker gloomily. 'The place is regularly besieged on Midsummer's eve.'

There was a battered old saddlebag close to the body.

'All right to look inside?' I asked.

Parker nodded. 'We've already checked. Nothing in there but a few old plants.'

I looked at the wilted greenery inside the saddlebag. 'Oak leaves and mistletoe,' I said. ' "They solemnise no sacrifice, nor perform any sacred ceremonies without branches and leaves thereof." '

I'd read the quotation during my recent researches and for some reason it had stuck. I looked round the ring of blank faces.

'The Roman historian Pliny,' I explained, 'writing about the druids.'

'Are you suggesting that this was some kind of druid sacrifice?' asked Chief Inspector Blane.

'I say, it's a possibility,' said Major Truscott excitedly. 'Maybe he broke the rules of some sacred order of druids, so some of his fellow druids brought him here and polished him off on the Slaughter Stone!'

'Are you serious?' demanded Inspector Parker. 'Because if I've got to start rounding up all the druids in the neighbourhood . . .'

'I don't think it's very likely,' I said. 'Mind you, the ancient druids were a pretty bloodthirsty lot. They used to burn people alive inside giant wickerwork figures. But, as far as I know, the modern-day druids are pretty harmless.'

Inspector Parker nodded in agreement. 'That's true enough. They let them in here sometimes to have a bit of a ceremony. They seem quite happy with a bit of marching about and chanting. Never seen any signs of bloodshed. Mind you, the ceremonies have mostly been put a stop to now.'

'Well, I think that explains what he was doing here,' I said. 'Are you saying that it's much harder to get permission now – to have a druid ceremony, I mean?'

Inspector Parker nodded. 'It all got out of hand. You should have seen the scrum in here on

Midsummer's eve.'

'That would be it, then,' I said. 'I bet this poor man was a mad-keen druid, desperate to perform a ceremony in the sacred circle. He couldn't get official permission, so he broke in – climbed over the fence, I expect. It's not all that high.'

Parker nodded. 'His old bike's propped up against the fence over there.'

'Well, all that seems clear enough,' said Dad briskly. 'I'm sure Matthew's theory is correct. The old boy broke in to perform some kind of un-authorised druid ceremony. Before he could even start – the oak and mistletoe were still in the sad-dlebag, remember – he stumbled on something that killed him.'

'But what?' asked Ms Alexander thoughtfully.

'That's what we're here to find out,' said Dad. 'Doctor Saville, you said there were some unusual features about this death?'

His moment of glory arrived at last, Doctor Saville bustled forward. He knelt by the body and started lecturing us like a group of students.

'Now, the obvious cause of death might seem to be the shattering of the skull – but beware of the obvious, ladies and gentlemen. In fact, the body has suffered some massive trauma, the grip of a force so powerful that the bones were pulverised.' He held up the old man's arm. It flopped horribly, as loose as a piece of spaghetti. 'I can't tell until I've done a full post-mortem, but I am convinced that this unknown force was the real cause of death.'

Dad took a little silvery gadget from his pocket – the Geiger counter I'd seen him use in Australia. He passed it gently to and fro over the body, and we heard a faint beeping.

He started lecturing us as well.

'I can add only one thing to Doctor Saville's most interesting remarks – with which I entirely agree. This body is radioactive.'

Everybody backed away from the body.

'It's all right,' said Dad. 'The radiation is extremely low-level. There's no danger from such brief exposure as this.' He turned to me. 'It's very similar to the kind of radiation we encountered in those craters in Australia.'

I nodded, lost in thought. The craters he was talking about had been used as landing places by alien ships over thousands of years.

Dad looked hard at me. 'Any observations to

offer, Matthew? You're our alien expert.'

I shook my head. 'There doesn't seem to be anything much to go on.'

'What about the effect of the weapon that killed the man?' asked Chief Inspector Blane. 'Have you seen anything like it before?'

I shook my head. 'It's certainly not the kind of weapon I saw in Australia – or in the Bermuda Triangle. That was more of a heat weapon. Things burst into flame, and people were charred into ashes.'

'They might have more than one kind of weapon,' said Dad. 'Just as we do.'

I nodded miserably. 'It's not the change of weapon that worries me, it's the change of attitude.'

'How do you mean?'

'The aliens I encountered weren't exactly benevolent, but they weren't murderers either. They fought back if they were attacked and they killed in self-defence. But, by and large, if you left them alone, they'd leave you alone.'

'Perhaps they feel themselves threatened in some way,' said Dad.

'What threat could this old man have been to

them? What's worrying me is – why have they suddenly become hostile?'

Chapter Three

THE STATION STONE

'Well,' said Chief Inspector Blane. 'What next?'

'I think we should let Doctor Saville get on with his post-mortem,' said Dad. 'The sooner we get some hard facts about the cause of death, the better. Meanwhile, I'd like to make a thorough examination of the site. You'll have to keep it closed for a while, I'm afraid.'

'How long?' asked Inspector Parker.

'Impossible to say. Several days, perhaps.'

'The public won't like it. It's out of season, I know, but a surprising number of people still turn up every day.'

'The public will have to put up with it,' said Blane.

Ms Alexander backed him up. 'We've already reinforced the heritage staff and their security firm with our own people. Stonehenge is closed to the public until further notice.'

Inspector Parker shook his head. 'If you say so. But it'll attract a lot of attention. You'll have media people down here in droves. What do we tell them?'

'Why don't you tell them there's a safety risk?' I suggested. 'Leak a story that one of the stones fell down and squashed someone, and let them think you're trying to cover it up.'

'Disinformation,' said Ms Alexander happily. 'Excellent idea! There's a great future for you in the intelligence business, young man.'

The waiting ambulancemen were sent for and the old man's shattered body was covered with a blanket and lifted on to a stretcher. Doctor Saville escorted it away, promising a preliminary post-mortem report as soon as possible. Major Truscott took himself off as well, asking to be kept informed of any developments.

Dad turned and looked at the circle of stones. 'Well, we'd better get started.'

'What are we looking for exactly?' asked Chief Inspector Blane.

'Anything!' said Dad. 'All we have so far is a theory about what the dead man was doing here.

What we really need to know is what killed him –
and why!'

A policeman – the one who'd tried to keep us
out – emerged from the tunnel and came up to
Inspector Parker. 'There's a Professor Mortimer
outside, sir. Says he's been doing excavation work
here.'

'Yes, I know him,' said Parker. 'Tell him we're
very sorry but the site is temporarily closed.'

'The thing is, sir, he saw the body being lifted
into the ambulance.'

'So?'

'Well he recognised the man, sir, says he knows
him well.'

'Right,' said Inspector Parker. 'Wheel him in!'

The policeman hurried away.

'You say you know this Professor Mortimer?'
asked Dad.

Parker nodded. 'He's a well-known local
archaeologist. Mad about Stonehenge, written
books about it. Even moved down here to be close
to the place. He had special permission from the
heritage people to work on the site.'

'Might be a useful bloke to have around,' I said.

Dad frowned. 'Why?'

'Presumably he's an expert on Stonehenge. He probably knows the place backwards. And if he's been working here just recently he'll know if anything is strange or out of place.'

'We'll see,' said Dad. I got the distinct feeling that he felt that one professor – him – was more than enough for any investigation.

The policeman returned with a tall, beaky-nosed character in a long tweed coat. He wore one of those tweed hats like an upside down flower-pot, jammed on to a mop of iron-grey hair. He had half-moon spectacles perched on the end of his nose, and he peered at us over them with bright blue eyes.

Inspector Parker made the introductions.

'Professor Mortimer – Professor Stirling, Matthew Stirling, Ms Alexander, Chief Inspector Blane. Colleagues, Professor Mortimer.'

Naturally enough, Mortimer homed straight in on Dad, professor to professor so to speak.

'Professor – Stirling, did you say? Forgive me, I thought I was familiar with most of my colleagues in the archaeological field but I don't seem to recall . . .'

Dad wasn't too pleased to be told that the

40

old boy had never heard of him, but he managed to be polite. 'No reason why you should. I'm an astro-physicist and several other things, but I make no claim to be an archaeologist – though I've dabbled a little even in that subject . . .'

Professor Mortimer cocked his head on one side like a curious bird. 'Not Professor James Stirling? The man who did such excellent work in the field of space travel?'

The atmosphere warmed up immediately, and Dad preened himself. 'You're very kind.'

'I've always taken a particular interest in your field, Professor Stirling. Strictly as an amateur, of course. My own work means I spend most of my time down in the mud, but occasionally I raise my eyes up to the stars! I'm delighted to meet you – especially here in a place where our two very different disciplines meet!'

'I'm delighted to meet you too, professor,' said Dad, and the two shook hands.

Ms Alexander and Chief Inspector Blane were watching all this with quiet amusement. Inspector Parker, however, was clearly getting fed up with this academic love-fest.

'I understand you know the identity of the

dead man, Professor Mortimer – the one you saw being put into the ambulance?'

'I most certainly do. I recognised the poor fellow immediately. What a shocking condition he was in! I've never seen anything like it. What happened to him?'

'That's what we're trying to find out,' said Parker. 'Well?'

Mortimer looked baffled. 'Well what?'

'Who was he?' asked Parker patiently.

'Oh, I'm sorry. His name was Grimble. Arthur Grimble. He was – or rather he desperately wanted to be – a druid.'

'Was he a member of The Ancient Order of Druids?' I asked.

'Over the years he had been a member of a number of such organisations,' said Mortimer. 'They all expelled him because of the extremity of his views. He was convinced that Stonehenge is a sacred temple, you see. All this . . .' Mortimer waved vaguely in the direction of the tunnel, the ticket-booth and the giftshop, '. . . all this was a kind of blasphemy to him. He thought that all tourists should be banned; that only true believers, such as himself, should be admitted.'

'I take it you don't share his views?' I asked. 'You don't think Stonehenge is a druid temple?'

Mortimer turned his bright blue eyes towards me. 'My dear boy, Stonehenge may well be many marvellous things. A Neolithic computer, a time machine, an astro-navigational device. But the one thing it is not, and never has been, is a druid temple!'

'How did you come to know Grimble?' I asked. 'Since you don't share his beliefs . . .'

'He sought me out,' said Mortimer simply. 'I have a certain local reputation, and he wanted to enlist me as an ally.'

'An ally in what?' asked Chief Inspector Blane.

'He had become obsessed with the idea that someone or something wanted to use Stonehenge for evil purposes. He was convinced that only through the performance of certain mystic druid ceremonies could the evil be averted. He came to me and asked for my assistance. I did my best to put him off. He wasn't the sort of person the authorities would ever grant access.'

'How did he react when you refused to help him?' asked Dad.

'He said he would perform the ceremonies

with or without my help. I assumed he meant to break in somehow. I warned him not to come here last night – or any other night – but he wouldn't listen. I suppose I should have informed the authorities of his plans, but I couldn't be sure that he really intended to carry them out – and besides, to be honest, I didn't have the heart. I was afraid of getting the poor old fellow into serious trouble. I take it he did break in – and came to grief somehow?'

'His body was found just here,' I said.

Mortimer knelt and examined the bloodstains on the stone. 'Poor fellow. I suppose he must have fallen and hit his head on the stone?'

'We're not sure,' said Chief Inspector Blane.

'We're about to make a thorough search of the site,' said Dad.

'Search?' Mortimer cocked his head in alarm. 'Search for what, may I ask?'

'For some clue as to what actually happened here,' said Dad. 'We'd be grateful for your help, Professor Mortimer.'

Professor Mortimer looked even more alarmed. 'Yes, of course. Though I'm at a loss to see exactly what . . .'

'You know the site better than anyone else here,' said Dad, cheerfully pinching my idea. 'If you could just tell us if you see anything unusual, anything that seems to have been disturbed.'

At this point Ms Alexander made her excuses and left, promising to keep in touch and return the next day if necessary. The cynical thought occurred to me that, as the risk of doing some real work got closer, our numbers were shrinking steadily. I said as much to Chief Inspector Blane while Dad and Inspector Parker were getting the search organised.

'Always the way,' he said cheerfully. 'On a sensitive case like this, you start off with top brass coming out of your ears. By the time you start doing the door-to-door or sorting through someone's dustbins, they've all melted away.'

'You're still here,' I pointed out.

'It's my job.'

'Which is?'

He gave me a surprised look – surprised at my cheek, I suppose – and then grinned. 'You might call it liaison. Case like this – well, it's got several levels to it. It's a suspicious death. Could be accident, could be murder, could even be suicide, though I admit that doesn't seem likely. Anyway, all that's the business of Inspector Parker and the local police.'

'Who resent any suggestion of interference?'

Blane smiled grimly. 'Yes, you could say that. Then again, Stonehenge is in the middle of a very sensitive area. There might just possibly be security aspects, so we get the funnies involved as well.'

'Funnies?'

'Spooks, spies, intelligence people, Ms Alexander's mob. Bunch of paranoids who think they're above the law and won't tell you the time of day without a security clearance.'

'And you're in the middle?'

'I'm in the middle. Now can I ask you something?'

'Go ahead.'

'This paranormal research department that your father runs . . . what is it exactly?'

'It's a department of a big scientific institute in America.' I didn't tell him the department had only been set up so the institute could get its hands on a fifty-million-dollar bequest from an eccentric millionaire obsessed by the paranormal.

Blane hesitated. 'There was some mention of UFOs – aliens. Is that why you're here?'

'I suppose so.'

'And these things exist? You've seen them?'

I hesitated, knowing he was going to think that I was some kind of nut, as crazy as the poor dead druid.

'Yes,' I said levelly. 'They exist and I've seen them.'

'But who are they? What do they want?'

'I don't know. I don't think anyone does.'

'Are they hostile?'

'They weren't when I encountered them. But now . . .'

He studied me thoughtfully. 'Well, you *seem* sane enough.'

'I am, I promise you. Talk to Dad if you get a chance. He accepts the existence of UFOs and aliens now – at least, I think he does – and he started out a bigger sceptic than you are.'

By now Inspector Parker had got the search underway. A dozen policemen were to search the Stonehenge site centimetre by centimetre. If they found anything of interest, they weren't to touch

47

it, but to call in Dad and Professor Mortimer.

I attached myself to Professor Mortimer, who was standing around looking lost. He was an interesting old bird and I wanted to know more about him.

Mortimer seemed glad to have someone to talk to. He pointed down to the flat stone where the body had been found. 'They call this the Slaughter Stone,' he said. 'A complete misnomer, of course.'

'More druid sacrifice stories?'

'I'm afraid so. People thought these bumps and hollows were made to hold the victims' blood. In fact, this is probably a fallen marker stone – it stood by the central causeway.'

I pointed to two more stones, well outside the main circle, one on either side of it, one fallen and the other still upright. 'What about those?'

'They're called the Station Stones. No one quite knows what their purpose was. Did you realise that the central axis of the monument lines up with the midsummer sunrise?'

Mortimer went on to tell me more about Stonehenge than I really wanted to know. Before long my head was spinning with sarsen circles, bluestones, trilithons (those were the pillars with a sort of crossbar stone on top) and the Aubrey Holes (a ring of burial pits discovered by some earlier archaeologist). Not to mention the Heel Stone and the central Altar Stone – another misnomer, according to Mortimer. He was very scornful of the druid temple theory, and of most other theories about Stonehenge as well. According to him, the real secret of Stonehenge was still waiting to be discovered.

'Some day the world will know,' he said. 'When my Great Work is complete.'

There was a fanatical gleam in his eyes. It was quite clear that, in his own way, he was just as obsessed with Stonehenge as the poor old dead druid had been. I wondered if his particular theories were any more sensible, and what the completed Great Work would reveal to the waiting world.

The lecture was interrupted by a shout from the policeman who was searching the area around the nearest Station Stone, the fallen one.

We all congregated round the stone and the young constable said, 'Don't know if it means anything, sir, but you said to report everything.'

'Well?' snapped Parker.

The policeman pointed. 'There are signs of digging here, around the base of the stone.'

'Looks as if something might have been buried there recently,' said Parker thoughtfully.

We all studied the freshly turned earth, wondering what, if anything, it meant.

The silence was broken by a nervous cackle of laughter from Mortimer. 'I'm afraid that is my responsibility, gentlemen. I got permission from the authorities for a limited amount of excavation and I've been working around this Station Stone. I beg you not to disturb the dig, it's in a very delicate state.'

After this false alarm the search resumed, but yielded only the odd cigarette carton and crisp packet left by careless tourists. Nothing very significant was found. In fact, the discovery of an old Coke bottle was pretty much the high spot of the search. Parker sent it off to be checked for bloodstains or fingerprints, but you could see his heart wasn't really in it.

It was beginning to get dark by now and, although Parker offered to rig up floodlights and go on with the search, we'd all had enough. We went back through the tunnel and congregated in the carpark, discussing arrangements for the next day.

Dad and I were to stay the night and he and Parker were discussing the best place for us to stay. I went up close to Dad and jabbed him in the ribs to get his attention.

'Never mind four-star comfort and luxury,' I hissed. 'Just make sure we stay somewhere close – in sight of Stonehenge. Trust me, it's essential!'

Dad frowned, and then nodded, and went on with the discussion. I slipped away in the gathering gloom and disappeared into the blackness of the tunnel. There was something I had to check out.

It was dark and sinister in the tunnel and, short as it was, I was glad to come out on the other side. Stonehenge loomed against the darkening sky.

I hurried over to the fallen Station Stone where the policeman had found signs of digging. I took the Geiger counter that I'd pick-pocketed from Dad during our brief conversation, and held it over the freshly turned earth. It started to bleep.

I took out my new Swiss Army knife and began

digging with the biggest blade. As I dug the bleep grew louder . . .

Before long, I managed to dig out a small hollow – and at the bottom of the hollow the blade struck something metallic.

I cleared away the earth to reveal a small glowing sphere . . .

Chapter Four

SIGNAL

I crouched in the dusk for a moment, staring at the glowing sphere. I'd expected to find it – at least, I'd expected to find *something* – but I still couldn't believe it was really there.

On a sudden impulse, I snatched up the sphere and thrust it deep into my anorak pocket. I filled in the hollow and moved away – just as Professor Mortimer came striding out of the tunnel. The long overcoat flapping round him made him look like some giant bat.

'You, boy, what are you doing?' he called. 'Are you interfering with my dig? What have you got there? Let me see!'

I stuck my hand into my pocket – my jeans pocket – and fished out a bunch of keys. 'I lost my keys when we were searching the site. They must have slipped out of my pocket.' I held up the bunch of keys. 'It's all right, I've found them again.'

'I don't believe you!'

He marched menacingly towards me and I was just preparing to leg it when a voice called out from the darkness behind him. 'Matthew, are you all right?'

Dad came out of the tunnel, and Professor Mortimer came to a sudden stop.

'I'm fine,' I said. 'I came back to look for my keys but I've found them now. Shall we be going?'

Dad looked incredulously at the sphere as it lay incongruously in the ash-tray on the desk in my hotel bedroom.

'It was most irresponsible of you, Matthew! Why did you just make off with it like that?'

'It seemed a good idea at the time,' I said feebly.

We were staying in a small village on Salisbury Plain, very close to Stonehenge. You could actually see Stonehenge close by from the windows of the inn, which satisfied me, and the village inn – it was called the Druid and Staff – was famous for its comfort and its cooking, which meant Dad was happy as well.

At least he had been happy, until I got him to come to my room after dinner and showed him the glowing sphere.

'Apart from anything else, it was an appallingly dangerous thing to do,' he said. 'Suppose that sphere is highly radioactive.'

'I only found very light radiation at the place where I found it,' I said. 'I thought I'd take a chance. After all, the citizens of Aberdeen absorb low-level radiation from their granite buildings every day.'

'Who told you that?' he demanded.

'You did, when we were out in Australia.'

'All right, all right,' grumbled Dad. 'All the same, I'd better test it.'

He started searching his pockets for his Geiger counter. 'Don't say I've lost the wretched thing!'

'Oh, sorry!' I fished the little device out of my pocket and handed it over. 'I borrowed it earlier,' I explained.

'I don't recall you asking . . .'

'I didn't ask.'

Giving me an outraged glare, Dad passed the device over the sphere, listened to the bleeps, and studied the readings.

'Well, you're right, fortunately for you! The radiation is low enough to be harmless, certainly for relatively short exposures.'

He put the gadget away and then gave me one of his stern looks. 'Now then, Matthew, kindly explain yourself. Why didn't you hand that sphere in to the authorities?'

'What would have happened if I had?'

He frowned. 'I don't know. I suppose they'd have sent it to some government laboratory for examination.'

'Exactly! And we'd never have seen it again. It would have vanished, like that alien spaceship material I found in Australia. Before long it would never have existed.'

'So you stole the sphere just to prove your theories about the extraterrestrial?'

'I didn't steal it!' I yelled. 'I'm the one who found it, remember? If I'd left things to you lot it would still have been sitting there under the Station Stone. I just thought we deserved to have a look at it first. A government laboratory will take ages. Then it'll be too late.'

'Too late for what?'

I paused. 'To be honest, I'm not sure. I've got a sort of . . . foreboding. A premonition, if you like.'

'What kind of premonition?'

'A feeling that something's about to happen at Stonehenge. Something important and urgent – and dangerous for Earth. We've just got to find out what's going on, and I don't think there's much time.'

Dad looked thoughtfully at me. 'This feeling of yours, Matthew . . . Do you think it has something to do with your previous . . . experiences?'

He was referring to the fact that on at least two previous occasions I had managed to achieve some kind of communication with the aliens. Not that I'd talked with them – they didn't talk, as far as I could see. This was more like some kind of mental link, an exchange of feelings and ideas.

'It might be,' I said. 'Maybe my mind became sensitised to them in some way. Maybe I'm just picking things up out of the air.'

'And maybe you're imagining it all,' said Dad.

As a scientist, he hates people forming what he calls airy-fairy theories without proper evidence.

I pointed to the glowing sphere in the ash-tray. 'I didn't imagine that!'

'Good point,' said Dad. 'All right, Matthew, I'm inclined to trust your instincts.' He picked up the sphere and studied it, turning it over in his hands. 'Though what I'm supposed to make of this thing without proper lab facilities . . . I suppose it might be some kind of signalling device.' He passed it over to me. 'Right now, your guess is as good as mine.'

I stared at the sphere, thinking hard – and felt it grow warm as if responding to the pressure of my mind. Suddenly it split into two joined halves, as if on some kind of central hinge.

The interior of the sphere was packed with intricate, jewel-like controls, and it pulsed steadily with an unearthly light.

'How did you do that?' asked Dad, amazed.

'I'm not sure. I just sort of . . . *thought* it open.'

Dad took the divided sphere and studied the instrument-packed interior intently.

'There's a sort of resemblance to the navigational instrumentation on a space-capsule – miniaturised, of course, and infinitely more complex and advanced. And as for the power source . . .' He shook his head despairingly. 'I think it probably is sending a signal, almost certainly on very precise, preset co-ordinates. But what signal, and to whom . . . ?'

He handed it carefully back to me. 'Here, you'd better think it shut again!'

I took the sphere and after a moment it closed in my hand. I put it carefully back in the ash-tray.

'Well, if that's our only lead . . .' said Dad. 'I honestly don't see what we can do with it except turn it over to the proper authorities.'

'It isn't our only lead,' I said. 'We've got Professor Mortimer as well.'

'You think he's involved?'

'I'm sure of it!'

'What makes you so certain? And don't you dare say it's just a feeling!'

'Well, it *is* a feeling,' I admitted. 'But there's a certain amount of circumstantial evidence as well.' I fished a guide to Stonehenge and neighbouring monuments out of my bag and turned to the diagram of Stonehenge in the front. 'Look, here's the point where our druid got over the fence, here's the Slaughter Stone where his body was found and here's the Station Stone where I found the sphere. All more or less in a straight line.'

'And what does that prove?'

'It doesn't exactly prove anything. But it seems very probable that our poor old druid got over the fence, got as far as the Slaughter Stone, and spotted something happening at the Station Stone – perhaps he saw the sphere being buried. Anyway, he called out and got zapped, and his body fell on to the Slaughter Stone. All this made enough noise to arouse the security people, and whoever killed him cleared off.'

Dad frowned. 'And you think Professor Mortimer did all this?'

'It's a possibility.'

'Mortimer couldn't possibly have made that sphere,' objected Dad. 'And how could he have exercised the unknown force that killed that poor man? Remember what Doctor Saville said about the bone structure being crushed.'

'Someone – some alien, even – could have given him the sphere,' I said. 'Just as they could have given him the weapon that killed the druid.'

Dad was losing patience – not that he ever had much in the first case. 'Really, Matthew, this is all pure speculation!'

'Not entirely,' I said. 'Look at what happened

this afternoon.'

'Well, what did happen?'

'To begin with, old Mortimer just happens to turn up at the crucial moment – and recognises a body being carried past him on a stretcher. A body which is covered by a blanket. There'd have been nothing to see.'

Dad frowned. 'Suspicious, perhaps, but far from conclusive. What do you think it means?'

'I think that Mortimer already knew Grimble was dead,' I said. 'I think he turned up to find out what was going on, and how much *we* knew. He used recognising the body as an excuse to get inside.'

'Anything else?'

'Plenty,' I said. 'As soon as the policeman spotted signs of digging around the Station Stone, Mortimer comes dashing up and says it was him all along.'

'Well?'

'I think he was lying,' I said. 'According to all my guidebooks, the area underneath the Station Stones was excavated years ago. There'd be no point in any more digging, and I doubt if the authorities would allow it. Besides, I had a long talk with Mortimer this afternoon. Although he's an archaeologist, his particular interest is the astronomical aspects of Stonehenge – and that involves measuring, not digging!'

'Still all speculation,' said Dad.

'Easy enough to find out,' I said. 'Call Inspector Parker and get him to check up on exactly what work Mortimer has permission to carry out at Stonehenge.'

With a look of weary resignation, Dad went over to the phone, took a notebook out of his pocket and dialled for an outside line. 'Inspector Parker? Forgive me for disturbing you, but I wonder if I could ask you to check up on something for me. It concerns Professor Mortimer and the work he's been doing at Stonehenge . . .'

Dad explained what we wanted to know, thanked Parker and put down the phone. 'He says he'll ring back.'

We sat looking at each other for a moment.

'Even if your theory proves correct,' said Dad at last, 'there's still the question of what we should do about it.'

'I've got an idea about that as well,' I said.

Dad groaned. 'That's exactly what I was

afraid of!'

Parker called back a few minutes later. Dad listened carefully then said, 'Thank you, that's most helpful.' He put down the phone and said, 'Well, you were quite right, Matthew. Professor Mortimer has been given permission to take measurements and to conduct certain stellar and lunar observations. There is absolutely no question of any digging being involved – in fact, it's specifically forbidden.'

I thought for a moment. 'Stellar and lunar – excellent. That fits in with my plans.'

Dad gave me a wary look. 'Which are?'

'I think that whatever was going on at Stonehenge was interrupted – first by the poor old druid turning up, then by all the fuss after his death. On top of that, I think Mortimer was suspicious of me today. He may even suspect that I've taken the sphere.'

'Go on,' said Dad resignedly.

'Stellar and lunar,' I said again. 'Stars and moon – which come out at night. In other words, Mortimer's got permission to be on the site at night-time. I think he'll go back there tonight to check up on the sphere – maybe finish whatever he started. I think we should go back over to Stonehenge and wait for him.'

'So, that's why you wanted a hotel close to Stonehenge. All right, Matthew, you seem to be running the show. But I insist that we let Inspector Parker know what's going on. If we're going to lie in ambush for Mortimer, I want plenty of police and security men close by – just in case he brings a few friends with him.' Dad nodded towards the glowing sphere. 'What about that? Do we take it with us?'

'And risk losing our only bit of evidence?' I shook my head. 'We'll leave it here. I'll wrap it in a pair of old socks and hide it in my bag.'

'Well, that should be enough to deter any marauding aliens,' said Dad. 'I'll ring Inspector Parker.'

'All right,' I said. 'But do me a favour.'

'What's that?'

I pointed to the sphere. 'Don't tell him, or any-one else, about that thing – not yet. We can hand it over afterwards. Please, Dad.'

'I don't like it – but if you insist . . .'

He picked up the phone.

Several hours later, I was lying flat on the grass behind a mound called the South Barrow, not far from the fallen Station Stone. Dad was on one side of me, Inspector Parker on the other. The circle of Stonehenge loomed in front of us, looking strangely sinister against the night sky.

All around us in the darkness, policemen and security guards ringed the entire perimeter. Only a bare minimum of working lights were switched on in the carpark and Stonehenge itself was shrouded in darkness.

'Do you really think he'll come?' whispered Dad.

I did my best to sound confident. 'Sure of it.'

'He may get in,' whispered Inspector Parker grimly. 'But he'll never get out.' The instructions were that if Professor Mortimer turned up at the gate he was to be admitted as usual. Even if he broke in, he was to be allowed to do anything he wanted to – anything except leave.

Stretched out beside me, Dad was getting impatient. 'How much longer, Matthew?' he hissed. 'I'm cold, I'm cramped and I'm bored. I want a large whisky and a warm bed.'

'We've only just got here,' I said. 'It's not even

midnight yet.'

'Well, how long are we going to wait?'

'As long as it takes.'

'Matthew, I warn you . . .'

'Tell you what,' I said. 'If he doesn't turn up by dawn we'll give up!'

Dad groaned.

'Sssh!' I hissed. 'I think someone's coming.'

We heard a voice from the tunnel. It was one of the regular security men. 'Are you sure you'll be all right, professor? I could switch on some lights for you?'

Then came Mortimer's voice. 'You're very kind, but please don't trouble yourself. I need to take a number of astronomical observations and the darkness is a positive advantage.'

'Right you are, sir, I'll leave you to it.'

A few minutes later, the tall figure of Professor Mortimer came striding out of the tunnel. We watched from our hiding-place as he strode swiftly over to the fallen Station Stone and began scrabbling beneath it. He seemed to be digging frantically, using some kind of trowel. Even from behind the South Barrow we could hear the hiss of disappointment and anger when he found that the sphere was gone.

He straightened up for a moment and appeared to be feeling in his pockets. Suddenly there was another glowing sphere in his hands.

I waited to see what he would do, but Inspector Parker seemed to feel that he'd waited long enough. He jumped to his feet and shouted, 'Torches, men! All right, professor, don't move!'

Torch-beams sprang out of the darkness, and suddenly Professor Mortimer was surrounded by a ring of police and security men.

He stood, motionless, the sphere glowing softly in his hand.

'There's no chance of escape, professor,' said Parker. 'Just hand that thing over and come with us. You've got a lot of questions to answer.'

Mortimer stood quite still for a moment. Then he raised his hand, holding the bright sphere up to the darkness.

A glowing disc of light came out of the sky. It hovered for a moment, directly over Mortimer's head.

With a yell of alarm, a security guard leaped forward. I suppose he must have intended to grab Mortimer, to stop him getting away.

A beam of light shot from the hovering disc. There was a blinding flash and the security guard screamed. The disc disappeared into the sky, and Mortimer vanished with it.

The circle of torchlight was empty – except for the crumpled body of the guard.

Chapter Five

ABDUCTION

Everything was a bit of a nightmare after that. People rushed around shouting and waving torches. They were still looking for the missing Professor Mortimer, unable to believe that they'd actually seen what they'd seen.

An ambulance was sent for and the body of the unfortunate security guard was carted off. His corpse showed the same horrible, boneless quality of the druid's body from the previous night. Tested with Dad's Geiger counter, it registered the same radioactivity.

Inspector Parker was furious, blaming himself for the poor security man's death.

Dad did his best to console him. 'It wasn't your fault, inspector. If anyone's, it was mine; I came up with the scheme. We'd have had to try to restrain Mortimer at some point. We just didn't realise what we were up against.'

It was generous of him to take all the blame, but it didn't make Parker, or me, feel any better.

The evening ended with an angry midnight conference in the site manager's office, which had been taken over for the occasion. All the top brass turned out again: Major Truscott, Chief Inspector Blane and the rather severe-looking Ms Alexander. All three of them were furious with Inspector Parker, and with us, for mounting the Mortimer operation without clearing it with them.

Inspector Parker defended himself heatedly. 'If we have to have a lengthy conference before every move, we'll never get anything done. Professor Stirling convinced me that Mortimer was implicated in a suspicious death and it was my duty to do my best to apprehend him.'

'Unfortunately, that best wasn't good enough,' said Major Truscott. 'What you failed to realise is that you're dealing with matters rather beyond the scope of a country policeman.'

Chief Inspector Blane came to the defence of his colleague. 'That's scarcely fair, Major Truscott. Inspector Parker acted for the best in very difficult circumstances. Isn't that so, Professor Stirling?'

'It most certainly is,' said Dad. He glared at Truscott. 'Do you really think you would have done any better? I've seen the attempts of the military mind to cope with this sort of thing. The only difference would have been a dead soldier instead of a dead security guard. Probably rather a lot of dead soldiers.'

Truscott went purple with rage and started to splutter.

'Gentlemen, please,' said Ms Alexander. 'No good will be done by these recriminations. Professor Stirling, I was responsible for involving you in this incident. With the greatest respect, I must say that I now believe it to have been a mistake. This sort of thing really ought to be left to professionals. I think it would be best if you were to return to London.'

When Dad's in a mildly cross and grumpy state – which he is most of the time – he tends to yell and carry on. It's mostly an act and, after a time, you ignore it. But when he's really mad he goes icy cold and very quiet.

For a moment he sat quite still. Then he said calmly, 'I wish you every success in your endeavours, ladies and gentlemen, whatever they may be. I'm sorry I wasn't able to be of more help. Matthew!'

Having pointed out that they didn't really know what they were doing, Dad rose to his feet and made a dignified exit, with me trailing behind.

He didn't say a word on the way out to the carpark. He didn't say anything until he was driving down quiet country lanes towards our village inn.

When he did speak it was only to mutter things like, 'Pompous military idiot!' and 'Jumped-up bureaucratic pen-pusher!' between clenched teeth. Suddenly he said loudly, 'Oh blast!'

'What's the matter?' I asked.

'That sphere you found. I was going to tell them about it and arrange to hand it in. Being dismissed by Ms Alexander made me so angry I forgot all about it. I suppose we really ought to pick it up at the hotel and take it back to them.'

I could tell by his tone that he didn't really mean it.

For some reason I was reluctant to part with the sphere myself. 'Pity to spoil a good dramatic exit,'

I said. 'Besides, think of the trouble we'll be in for not handing it over before.'

Dad thought about it. He hates being in the wrong, and I could see he didn't relish giving Truscott and Ms Alexander another good reason to tick him off. He came to a decision.

'All right, we'll hang on to it. I'll take it back to London. I can get access to first-class laboratory facilities there. I'll work on the thing myself. I'm quite as well qualified to investigate alien technology as anyone they'll have on their staff. Better, probably. When I've worked out its purpose, I'll send them a copy of my report.' Suddenly cheerful, he grinned at me. 'There could be a Nobel prize in this, my boy!' Dreaming of sweet scientific revenge, Dad drove happily along.

Although I was glad to see him cheering up, I wasn't feeling nearly so optimistic myself. There were just too many unanswered questions.

What was Mortimer's link with the aliens? Or was he an alien himself? What was the purpose of the glowing spheres, and why was it so important to bury them beneath Stonehenge? And why were the remote, detached aliens I'd encountered before now so ready to kill?

I was still mulling over all these questions when I became aware of a light coming from the sky behind us. I turned my head and saw a glowing disc in the sky just behind the car.

It was following us.

What was so weird was that it was all so familiar. It was a classic UFO sighting, a Close Encounter of the First Kind. The car on the lonely road, the light in the sky that seems to follow it, the terrified passengers. I'd read about it often when I'd been researching UFOs, and now it was happening to me.

I tapped Dad on the shoulder. 'Look behind you. We've got company.'

'I know,' said Dad, 'I can see it in the mirror. It's probably just . . .'

'A passing plane, a weather balloon, or the lights of the planet Venus,' I yelled. 'Come off it, Dad. Try believing your own eyes. It's a flying saucer and it's after us. It looks very like the thing that came and rescued Mortimer.'

'I'll shake it off,' said Dad. He put his foot down and we began zooming along the narrow lane.

'Don't be so daft,' I shouted. 'You can't outrun

a UFO, even in this thing.'

'What do you suggest I do, then?'

'Make for Salisbury, that's the nearest big town. UFOs don't usually land in busy high streets.'

We sped along the narrow lanes for a while and suddenly the following light disappeared.

'There you are,' said Dad. 'Relax, Matthew. Whatever it was, we've lost it!'

The glowing disc appeared in the sky directly ahead of us.

It descended with terrifying speed, apparently heading straight for the car. With a shout of alarm, Dad swung the car to the left to avoid it. We crashed through a hedge and our off-road vehicle, really off the road for once, bounced across what felt like a ploughed field.

But it was no use. Once again the glowing disc seemed to drop from the sky directly ahead of us. We drove straight into the glowing radiance and I lost consciousness.

I awoke some time later, feeling bruised, stiff and thoroughly uncomfortable. Most of all, I was scared. I knew the next scene in the UFO scenario all too well.

Cautiously, I opened my eyes. I expected to find myself strapped on to an operating table, with glowing-eyed aliens looking curiously down at me, sinister-looking instruments in their hands.

Instead, I saw the interior of the Land Tourer, illuminated by pale moonlight. I was still in exactly the same place.

'Dad!' I croaked. 'Dad, are you all right?'

There was no answer – and for a very good reason. When I turned my head I saw that there was no one in the driving seat.

I told myself that he had recovered consciousness before me and gone off to fetch help. But would he have gone without trying to revive me, without making quite sure I was all right?

It didn't seem likely.

Wouldn't he have left a note at the very least? I looked all over the dashboard. There was no note to be seen.

Cautiously I got out of the Land Tourer. We were in the middle of a ploughed field. In the moonlight I could see the ruts made by our wheels, running from the point where we'd left the road to the point where we'd stopped moving. I got a torch from the glove compartment and looked all round the Land Tourer. My feet made deep marks in the soft earth. But, apart from my own, there were no footprints.

No footprints at all.

Dad hadn't walked away from the crash, he'd been taken away.

He'd been abducted.

I followed the wheel-ruts back to the road and then walked along the lane towards the inn. The moonlight was fairly bright and I didn't really need the torch. Luckily, there wasn't very far to go. We'd been almost back at the village when the abduction happened.

The little inn was all locked up when I arrived, but they'd given us both front door keys so there was no problem about getting in. I opened the front door as quietly as I could and crept upstairs to my room.

I went to the bathroom and splashed my face with cold water.

I drank several glasses of cold water from the toothbrush glass.

Then I went to my old canvas travel bag, which was still sitting where I'd left it on the end of the bed, and fished out the spare shirt rolled up in the bottom. I unrolled the shirt – old socks had seemed disrespectful somehow – and revealed the glowing sphere.

I sat cradling it in my palms and wondered what to do next.

On the face of it, I supposed it was obvious. I ought to call the authorities and tell them what had happened.

The authorities! Major Truscott. Ms Alexander, who'd already dismissed us from the case. True, Chief Inspector Blane and Inspector Parker might be more sympathetic. But would any of them believe me? And even if they did, what could they do?

After all, UFO-abduction victims were never *found*. How could they be? Sometimes – but not always – they just turned up again of their own accord.

I remembered the story about the married couple abducted near Niagara Falls. They arrived home without realising anything had happened at all – until they discovered that several hours were unaccountably missing from their lives.

Then there was the young man who had

disappeared from a logging camp in Oregon. His co-workers said they'd *seen* him being abducted by a UFO. The authorities suspected them of murdering him. The missing man turned up several days later, with no memory of what had happened to him.

In both cases, it took hypnosis to restore the memory of abduction.

In the course of my research, I'd read about hundreds of such cases. Some I'd believed, others not. Now I was caught up in an alien abduction myself – and who was going to believe me?

Some alien abductees returned little the worse for their experiences. Others seemed mentally and physically scarred for life. I wondered where Dad was, and what was happening to him.

I wondered when – and if – I would ever see him again.

There was, I decided, really only one thing to do. I'd call the authorities and hand over the sphere. I'd tell them what had happened to Dad.

Then I'd wait for him to turn up again. It was a miserable prospect, but it seemed to be the only one on offer. Dad's notebook with Parker's number was still by the telephone. I reached for the phone – and just before I touched it, it rang!

I snatched up the receiver. 'Yes?'

For a moment there was silence, broken only by a strange electronic crackling. Then Professor Mortimer's voice said, 'You have the hyper-navigational sphere.'

I tried hard to keep my voice steady. 'Do I?'

'It was not beneath the Station Stone. You must have taken it. Your father does not have it – but we have your father.

'All three spheres are needed for the Transition. Time is short now. Bring the sphere to Stonehenge before dawn.'

The line went dead.

Professor Mortimer's voice had been calm and logical, as if he were pointing out the only possible thing to do. And, of course, he was right.

There was no need for threats. The simple fact that they had Dad was enough.

I sat for a moment studying the glowing sphere. The hyper-navigational sphere, he'd called it. One of the three essential for the Transition – whatever that was.

It didn't seem likely that the plans of Mortimer and his alien friends were going to be of much benefit to planet Earth.

Did I have the right to risk millions of lives simply to save the life of my own father?

Did I have any alternative?

I stared at the sphere and gave it a kind of mental push.

The two halves slid smoothly open and I stared at the complex miniature controls within.

All at once I knew what I had to do.

Chapter Six

TRANSITION

I tiptoed out of the sleeping inn and made my way round to the back. I'd noticed an old bike in the yard and I decided that since this was a national – in fact, a planetary – emergency, I was justified in borrowing it.

I wheeled the bike round to the front of the inn and wobbled off down the lane. I was in luck. The bike was old and creaky, but it worked. Even the lights worked in a flickering fashion, powered by an ancient dynamo attached to the back wheel.

I pedalled steadily towards Stonehenge, thinking about the old druid who'd done the same thing just a few nights ago.

I hoped I wasn't going to end up the same way.

Like the old druid, I cycled as near to Stonehenge as I could, and then got off and pushed my bike up to the fence.

Like him, I leaned the bike against the fence, climbed up on to the saddle and scrambled over to the other side.

I dropped down into the grass and waited, looking around me for signs of movement. I could hear quiet voices in the distance, and I saw the flash of a torch on the other side of the circle and the glow of a cigarette in the darkness.

There were certainly security men patrolling, but they didn't seem to be standing shoulder to shoulder as they had been earlier. My guess was that most of the extra security staff had been dismissed. Maybe the authorities thought that the crisis was over, at least for the time being.

A fat lot they knew about it.

I got up and moved slowly towards the towering circle of stones, passing between them until I reached the central Altar Stone.

Professor Mortimer stepped out of the shadows, a glowing sphere in his hand. How he got there, heaven knows – the same way I had, perhaps. Or perhaps his alien friends had helped him. 'You have the hyper-navigational sphere?' he hissed.

A single-minded chap, old Mortimer.

I took the sphere from my pocket and held it up.

'Give it to me.'

I shook my head. 'Not until I see my father, alive and well.'

'I shall take it from you.' He rushed through the darkness towards me.

I backed away and held the sphere up, close to the nearest stone pillar. 'If you or anyone else even tries, I'll smash this thing to pieces.'

Mortimer froze. 'No! You cannot destroy it – but you might jar the mechanism, the preset co-ordinates are delicate . . . Navigation in and out of hyperspace is incredibly complex.'

I was glad to hear it.

'Then let me see my father.'

'It is not possible.'

'Here and now, alive and well,' I said. 'Your friends took him, they can bring him back.'

Suddenly Mortimer laughed. 'Very well, why not? It is time to let these fools see what they are dealing with!'

He held up the sphere – and suddenly the disc of light I'd seen before was hovering over Stonehenge.

A beam of light shot from the disc, striking the Altar Stone. The beam spread and spread, like an ever-expanding spotlight, until all of Stonehenge was bathed in a circle of light.

The circle drove back the security men until they were all held outside its rim. Stonehenge was enclosed in a dome of light, with nobody inside but me and Mortimer.

'A simple forcefield,' said Mortimer. 'Stonehenge is ours!'

The air shimmered and, suddenly, Dad lay on the grass beside me. I bent down to examine him. He seemed perfectly well and sound asleep.

'The sphere,' said Mortimer.

I handed it over.

The air shimmered again, and a new form stood beside Mortimer.

It was an alien form, but not the kind of alien I knew. It was taller and thinner, black rather than silver-clad, the skin a darker shade of greeny-grey, the face more rounded, the slanted eyes a more vivid green. It held a glowing sphere in its hand.

I made an attempt at mental communication of the kind that had worked before. Who are you? I thought. What do you want?

There was no response. Just a blank mental wall of anger and hate.

Suddenly, the blindingly obvious struck me with a dull thud. It wasn't just a matter of a different kind of weapon. We were dealing with a different kind of alien. This particular specimen had nothing in common with the aliens I had encountered earlier. It didn't help matters, but it was a relief all the same.

Mortimer didn't seem to have any problem in communicating. 'Excellent,' he said. 'Now it is time for the three hyper-navigational spheres to be put in place.'

I waited beside Dad as Mortimer put his own sphere next to the fallen Station Stone, and the one I'd given him beside the Station Stone on the other side of the circle. The alien took its glowing sphere to a place on the far side of the circle – the place, I later learned, where the third Station Stone had once stood.

Mortimer and the dark alien returned to the centre of the stone circle.

Suddenly, the stones of Stonehenge began to glow. Electricity crackled from stone to stone. Ghostly stones, the long-missing pillars and crossbeams appeared and glowed with an unearthly light.

Just for a moment, I saw the complete Stonehenge, the Stonehenge of thousands of years ago.

'Now you see the true purpose of Stonehenge!' said Mortimer. He babbled on but I wasn't really listening. My attention was taken up by the shocking sight overhead.

An enormous spaceship, bristling with weapons, was appearing over Stonehenge, appearing above the smaller hovering disc.

Shadowy, semi-transparent at first, the ship seemed to be struggling to emerge from another dimension.

Suddenly, there was an explosion of light at the base of the far Station Stone – the one where *my* sphere had been placed. More explosions followed at the second and third Station Stones.

The flow of power between the other stones seemed to falter. There was a wild crackling, a blinding burst of light and the giant spaceship shimmered and disappeared.

'What has happened?' howled Mortimer. 'Something has gone wrong.' He turned to me. 'This is your work. What did you do?'

'I sabotaged the sphere I gave you back,' I said. 'I damaged it, just a little, enough to stop it working properly. I think it blew a fuse.'

'Do you realise what you have done?' screamed Mortimer. 'The mother ship and the rest of the invasion fleet are trapped in hyperspace. They are lost between the dimensions. They can never emerge.'

'Good,' I said. 'Your plan has failed. The invasion is cancelled.'

The black-clad alien turned to face Mortimer. It stretched out its hand, a beam of light shot out, and Mortimer screamed and crumpled to the ground.

It was the penalty for failure.

The alien swung round to me. Curiously enough, I wasn't afraid. I'd won. The alien invasion had been defeated. My death didn't seem important now.

Then it happened, just as I'd seen it happen in Australia not long ago. There was a kind of silent boom, reality shimmered and a giant glowing sphere was hovering over Stonehenge.

A beam of light shot out and the glowing disc vanished in a silent explosion.

Another beam and the black-clad alien glowed brightly and vanished into dust.

A doorway in the sphere opened and a ramp came down. A slender, silvery figure emerged and stretched out a hand in greeting. It was the alien I'd met in Australia, and again beneath the Bermuda Triangle. It was an old friend.

Our fingers touched for a moment and we . . . communicated.

Some time later, how long I'm not really sure, the silvery figure went back up the ramp and the glowing disc disappeared. The forcefield round Stonehenge disappeared as well, and baffled policemen and security guards flooded on to the site.

I knelt beside Dad, who opened his eyes and said, 'Matthew? What the hell's going on here?'

'That's a very good question,' I said.

Later still, another conference was held in the site manager's office. It was very different in tone from the one held earlier. This time, I had the floor, and every word I said was listened to with fascinated attention.

'I'm going to tell you what I think has been happening,' I said wearily. 'You can believe it or not, just as you please. I don't care to argue about it. Is that clear?'

'Absolutely,' said Ms Alexander.

Inspector Parker, Chief Inspector Blane and even Major Truscott nodded agreement.

Dad gave me a satirical look and said, 'Do go on, Matthew.'

'Right,' I said. 'Well, as far as I can make out, it goes like this. Thousands of years ago an alien race, perhaps several alien races, visited Earth. They left monuments behind, the Easter Island statues, the pyramids – and Stonehenge. But Stonehenge was different from all the others. Amongst other things, it was a navigational beacon, a way for alien ships to find their way out of hyperspace to reach the Earth.'

'For the benefit of any non-scientists amongst this purely *professional* assembly . . .' said Dad. (He dearly loves getting his own back.) 'Permit me to explain that travel to and from the stars is only conceivable if we postulate the existence of something called hyperspace – a dimension where space folds in upon itself, enabling the

90

immeasurably long distances between two stars to be crossed in finite time. Navigation in hyper-space, if it exists, would be a matter of incredible complexity. I'm sorry, Matthew, do go on.'

I went on. 'Time passed; thousands of years went by. The aliens left Earth and the secret of Stonehenge was forgotten. About fifty years ago Earth was rediscovered. Alien ships began visiting us again. Some, like the aliens I've encountered before, were simply curious. Others, like the aliens we've been having problems with here, were interested in conquest. They sent a scout ship to Earth, made contact and found a human sympathiser in Mortimer.

'I imagine they won him over by promising to reveal ancient knowledge. He was so desperate to know the truth about the history of Stonehenge that he was prepared to betray humanity for it. With his help, the invading aliens tried to reactivate Stonehenge as a hyperspace beacon. I think they wanted to bring an invasion fleet out of hyperspace. As you've just seen, they failed.'

'Thanks to you, Matthew,' said Dad.

'Only partly,' I said. 'The other aliens, the ones we encountered in Australia and in the Bermuda

Triangle, are opposed to conquest. They come here only to observe. At the last minute, they intervened to help me. Just as there's more than one kind of human, there's more than one kind of alien. Some of them aren't necessarily hostile. They may even be on our side. It's worth remembering that.'

That was more or less the end of it all. Nobody really knew for sure what had happened, but everyone was convinced that Dad and I had saved Earth from some awful catastrophe, and they were properly grateful.

Ms Alexander even said that if benevolent aliens did reappear on Earth, humanity would need an ambassador. She was kind enough to say that I was the only possible candidate for the post.

I said I'd let her know.

Later that morning, Dad and I were back in the Kamikaze Land Tourer, now retrieved from the ploughed field, heading back towards London. Tired as we were, we felt we couldn't stand the excitements of country life any longer.

I reminded Dad that he would find it difficult to maintain his role as a sceptic. He was now a genuine alien abductee. He could have regressive hypnotic therapy, write a book and appear on television chat shows describing his terrible experiences.

He didn't seem to think much of the idea.

'I don't know what happened between my leaving the car and turning up at Stonehenge, and I don't want to know,' he said.

'You don't know what memories you might be missing,' I said. 'A young Mexican farmer swears he was abducted and taken to a spaceship where a beautiful lady alien made mad, passionate love to him. What you might call a Close Encounter of the Fifth kind.'

'That will be quite enough of that, Matthew,' said Dad severely. 'I imagine I was simply kept in some kind of alien deep-freeze. Whatever my actual experiences may have been, I certainly don't intend to discuss them on breakfast television. I should be grateful if we could consider the subject closed. As far as I'm concerned, we've finished with UFOs and aliens.'

'Fine by me,' I said. 'The only thing is . . . have the UFOs and aliens finished with us?'